Do... ...ny?

By Da...

Illustr...

KT-511-583

Renew by phone or online
0845 0020 777
www.bristol.gov.uk/libraries
Bristol Libraries

PLEASE RETURN BOOK BY LAST DATE STAMPED

BR100

Ho

23304 Print Services

Bristol Libraries

1801690929

First Edition 2013

Text copyright © 2013 Dawn May

Illustrations copyright © 2013 Phil Goss.

Story by Dawn May. Illustration by Phil Goss.

All rights reserved. No part of the publication may be reproduced,

stored in or introduced into a retrieval system, or transmitted, in any

form, or by any means (electronic, mechanical, photocopying,

recording or otherwise).

With special thanks to

Sophia Duffy for her infinite patience and

valuable advice on all the technicalities of self publishing.

You are a gem.

ISBN: 978-1-291-53128-2

For Luca

Jake's granny has Parkinson's.
But it doesn't hurt, she says.

Sometimes, Jake and Granny
go for long walks.

They find leaves ...

and stones ...

and bugs ...

and snails ....

Granny has a book and they find out about them in there. That's on days when Granny can't go for long walks.

But it doesn't hurt, she says.

Sometimes Jake and Granny
go cycling.

They see birds and mice and sometimes slow worms - and once they saw a rat ....

Jake likes to go swimming
and his granny does, too

What a lot of splashing - oops -
better stop.

Stop it, Granny!

Can you hit a ball Granny?

Not like that!

Today, Jake and Granny are going to the seaside.

Look at all the shells
they've found.

Who used to live
in here?

Sometimes, Jake feels sad for Granny.
Granny can't play today.

But it doesn't hurt,
she says.

Jake's granny has Parkinson's,
but she can still ...

... go for walks

... and go on cycle rides

... and go for a swim

... and have a game of tennis

... and go to the seaside.

Jake's granny makes him laugh.

And, sometimes, *that* hurts.

Coming Soon

I'll do it, Granny

Steady on, Granny

Cheer up, Granny

Can we talk about it?

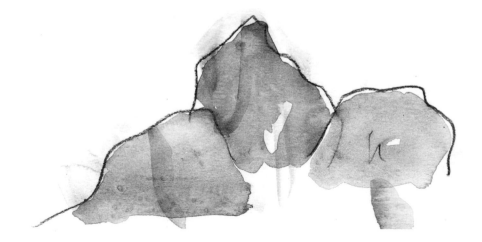